The Curse
Of
Sherlock Holmes

By Dhanil Ali

Paperback ISBN 9781780923772
ePub ISBN 9781780923789
PDF ISBN 9781780923796

Published in the UK by MX Publishing
335 Princess Park Manor, Royal Drive, London, N11 3GX
www.mxpublishing.com

Cover layout and construction by
www.staunch.com

Dedicated to the memory of Jeremy Brett.

The Curse of Sherlock Holmes

A Play In Two Acts

CAST

Jeremy Brett / Sherlock Holmes   Actor/ The Baker Street detective

Professor Doran   Female therapist, late 20's,

Professor Moriarty [Off]   Arch nemesis of Sherlock Holmes

John Watson [Off]   Biographer, friend and confidante of Sherlock Holmes

ACT 1

SCENE: PRIVATE HOSPITAL ROOM

SFX

THE SOUNDS OF EVERYDAY HOSPITAL EVENTS - THE CLATTERING OF A TROLLEY, A CRY OF DISTRESS, COUGHING. A TELEPHONE RINGS OUT.

*ON STAGE - THE DOOR OPENS SLOWLY. ENTER **JEREMY**. HE IS DRESSED IN LIGHT FLANNEL TROUSERS, WHITE SHOES, A MUSTARD COLOURED V-NECK SWEATER OVER WHICH IS DRAPED A MULTI COLOURED SCARF. HIS ENSEMBLE IS COMPLETED BY A WALKING CANE. HE IS RELUCTANT TO ENTER FULLY AND HOVERS WITH HIS BACK TO THE DOOR. APPEARS UNIMPRESSED. PLACES HIS FINGERS TOGETHER AND THEY FORM A TRIANGLE.*

JEREMY

Is this heaven or is this hell?

SURVEYS THE ROOM AS IF LOOKING FOR THE DANGERS IN A MINEFIELD. HIS EYES REST ON THE LAMP.

Ha!

HE DARTS TO THE LAMP AND HOLDS HIS HANDS BESIDE IT IN THE MANNER OF A MAGICIAN. REMOVES THE SCARF FROM HIS SHOULDERS AND PLACES IT OVER THE LAMPSHADE. HE STANDS BACK TO ADMIRE THE EFFECT. A PIROUETTE ENDS WITH A LONG SIGH. CLAPS HIS HANDS TOGETHER WITH GLEE. LISTENS. SLIGHT GRIMACE.

Acoustics – fair.

PLACES HIS HANDS TO HIS HEAD AND REALISES HE HAS FORGOTTEN SOMETHING.

My case!

SPRINGS TO THE DOOR AND OPENS IT. HE POPS HIS HEAD OUT AND BARKS INSTRUCTIONS. POLITELY.

Would you be so kind as to bring my case to me?
[CLOSES DOOR] Thank you!

JEREMY SITS ON THE BED. HIS EYES ARE DRAWN TO THE HIGH BACKED LEATHER CHAIR IN THE CORNER. CRANES HIS NECK AS HE SURVEYS THE ROOM.

All the charm of an open sewer. *[DISMISSIVE WAVE]* A snake pit, a veritable snake pit! *[AFTER A SERIES OF FACIAL GESTURES]* I need a cigarette. I will have a cigarette after which I will be able to do battle with my wiliest adversary.

DRAWS HIS KNEES UP TO HIS CHIN IN ICONIC HOLMES POSE.

I cannot function without my cigarettes – after all – this may well be a three pack problem.

GRUNTS. FACIALLY, HE LETS THE AUDIENCE KNOW THAT THE REMARK WAS CHEAP. ROCKS BACK AND FORTH GENTLY.

SFX
SOUNDS OF VICTORIAN LONDON.

JEREMY PLACES HIS HANDS OVER HIS EARS TO BLOCK OUT THE SOUND. HE DARTS TO THE DOOR AND BEGINS TO BANG ON IT.

JEREMY
[SHOUTING] My case if you please!

SFX
SOUNDS OF VICTORIAN LONDON FADE.

JEREMY UNCOVERS HIS EARS. LISTENS. HE WALKS TO THE MIRROR AND PEERS IN IT FOR SEVERAL SECONDS. TOUCHES HIS FACE.

JEREMY
[PATTING CHIN] Jowls. I have discovered jowls.

LOOKS FORLORN. TAKES A FLOWER FROM THE VASE AND READS THE ATTACHED CARD. IT APPEARS FROM THE LOOK ON HIS FACE THAT THE

CARD MEANS NOTHING TO HIM. DISMAYED. RESTS HIS LEFT ARM ON MIRROR AND PLACES HIS HEAD AGAINST IT. DISCARDS IT BY DROPPING IT TO THE FLOOR. SMELLS THE FLOWERS. RETURNS TO THE MIRROR AND EXAMINES HIS EYES.

> I am tired.

HOLDS BOTH EDGES OF THE MIRROR. STARES INTENTLY AT HIS REFLECTION. TILTS HIS HEAD TO THE LEFT THEN TO THE RIGHT. REPEATS THIS SEVERAL TIMES. APPEARS HE IS TRYING TO EVADE HIS IMAGE. DANCES LEFT AND RIGHT WITHOUT LETTING GO OF THE MIRROR. HIS REFLECTION FOLLOWS. BECOMES WILDER. PANICS. HIDES BELOW THE MIRROR WITH HIS BACK TO THE WALL. HIS BREATHING IS RAPID. SITS ON THE EDGE OF THE BED.

SFX
MORIARTY LAUGHTER.

JEREMY
> Whom the gods wish to destroy they first make mad.

SFX
MORIARTY LAUGHTER FADE.

***JEREMY** LOOKS TO THE HIGH BACKED LEATHER CHAIR. HIS GLARE IS VICIOUS. HE POINTS A THREATENING FINGER TOWARDS IT.*

HOLMES
> I will deal with you presently, my friend. Make no mistake for today I am your equal!

*THE DOOR OPENS. ENTER **PROFESSOR DORAN**. **JEREMY'S** FACE BREAKS INTO A WIDE BEAMING SMILE AS SHE APPROACHES.*

DORAN
> Jeremy?

JEREMY
> Ah, doctor *[RISING]* you caught me in repose.

***JEREMY** MOVES TOWARDS **DORAN** INTENDING TO SHAKE HER HAND.*

DORAN

[SMILING] It's actually Professor –

JEREMY

[ALARMED] Professor?

JEREMY REMOVES HIS HAND. HIS EYES DART TO THE HIGH BACKED LEATHER CHAIR. HE RUNS HIS HANDS THROUGH HIS HAIR TO DISGUISE THE FACT THAT HE WAS ABOUT TO SHAKE HANDS. BEGRUDGING SMILE.

I see. Please forgive me. I interrupted you when you were on the verge of telling me your name.

*MAKES HAND GESTURE TO HURRY **DORAN** ALONG.*

DORAN

It's Doran.

JEREMY

[CLAPS HIS HANDS TOGETHER AND SMILES] Ha! Doran! The Noble Bachelor!

DORAN

[CONFUSED] Pardon me?

JEREMY

[WAVES HIS HAND DISMISSIVELY] Fear not 'Professor' it is my way. It was a literary – oh, never mind.

JEREMY SITS ON THE EDGE OF THE BED. POINTS TO THE CHAIR BESIDE IT.

DORAN

[SITTING] Is the room ok?

JEREMY

Adequate.

DORAN

These rooms are a little sparse.

JEREMY

Yes.

DORAN NOTICES THE SCARF COVERING THE LAMPSHADE. GETS UP AND REMOVES IT. GIVES IT TO JEREMY.

DORAN

A safety precaution.

JEREMY LOOKS STONE FACED. THERE IS A LULL.

JEREMY

I see.

DORAN

Well, I just popped in to see if there was anything you needed.

JEREMY

[CORRECTING] Required!

DORAN

[UNCOMFORTABLY] Yes. Required.

JEREMY

My case if you please!

DORAN

Your case? Hasn't it been brought in yet?

JEREMY

[OPEN ARMS] As you can see.

DORAN

Well, I'll get on to it right away. *[OFFERS TO SHAKE JEREMY'S HAND. JEREMY TURNS HIS BACK]* Well, if there's anything else –

JEREMY

You have a propensity when nervous to begin sentences with

the word 'well.' I would look into that.

DORAN

[UNCERTAIN] Ok.

JEREMY

[ICILY] Goodbye!

DORAN

[EXITING] Well, I'll be back in a minute or two and we can have a little chat.

JEREMY

[SARCASTICALLY] Be still my beating heart.

DORAN

Bye. *[EXITS]*

JEREMY SITS ON THE BED. PULLS SEVERAL FACES. HE PLACES HIS HANDS UNDER HIS LEGS. HIS EYES WANDER AROUND THE ROOM IN THE WAY THAT A SMALL CHILD WOULD SURVEY NEW SURROUNDINGS. HE SINGS QUIETLY.

JEREMY

[SINGING] I could have danced all night, I could have danced all night, And still have asked for more, I could have – *[FORGETS LYRIC. CONTINUES BY HUMMING. FIZZLES OUT]*

SFX

KNOCK ON DOOR.

JEREMY

Coming!

JEREMY SPRINGS TO THE DOOR. OPENS IT. AN UNSEEN PERSON HANDS HIM HIS CASE. HE FORCES A SMILE.

Thank you! You are too kind!

SHUTS DOOR ABRUPTLY. THROWS CASE ONTO BED. OPENS IT. LID OBSCURES CONTENTS FROM AUDIENCE. HE SEARCHES THROUGH HIS BELONGINGS. STOPS.

Humph! No cigarettes! I must have my nicotine!

*ROOTS THROUGH CASE AGAIN. SOMETHING MAKES HIM SMILE A DEVILISH SMILE. HE PRODUCES A FRAMED PHOTOGRAPH. PLACES IT ON THE TABLE. IT IS A PORTRAIT OF THE ACTRESS **GAYLE HUNNICUT** AS **IRENE ADLER**. HE ADMIRES IT. SITS ON THE BED AND PLACES HIS HANDS BENEATH HIM WHILE HIS EYES ARE STILL FIXED ON THE FRAMED PHOTOGRAPH. PLACES PHOTOGRAPH ON TABLE.*

SFX

SOUNDS OF VICTORIAN LONDON.

JEREMY *PLACES HIS HANDS OVER HIS EARS. SOUNDS GROW LOUDER. BURIES HIS FACE IN THE PILLOWS AND CRIES OUT.*

SFX
SOUNDS OF VICTORIAN LONDON FADE.

JEREMY *UNCOVERS HIS EARS.*

MORIARTY
Your presence is heartening. I knew you would come.

JEREMY *DASHES TO THE DOOR AND PLACES HIS BACK AGAINST IT. HIS GAZE IS FIXED ON THE HIGH BACKED LEATHER CHAIR.*

If you are here simply as a spectator then kindly close the door on your way out. You can peer though the bars as do my captors.

HOLMES
You look – older – unwell.

MORIARTY
We are finite and cannot stop the march of time.

HOLMES
There is an unsightly pallor *[POINTS TO HIS EYES]* around the eyes. You look cold.

MORIARTY

I am cold! Do you think that these rags befit a man of my standing?

HOLMES

I must admit; they do look a little threadbare.

MORIARTY

Please – do not concern yourself. I predict an upturn in my fortune any time now.

HOLMES

Do not – count on that!

MORIARTY

There is little you can do to halt the inevitable landslide that will engulf you.

HOLMES

That a man of your mental prowess is reduced to this weighs heavily upon me regardless of our past encounters.

MORIARTY

A waste of valuable thought processing; besides; interested parties will soon see that my liberty is restored. I assure you that this predicament is but a temporary hiatus. It amuses me that you are as much a prisoner as I.

HOLMES

No, no, 'Mr' Moriarty! I am at liberty to leave whenever I wish.

MORIARTY

You have that in writing?

HOLMES

Tut. *[APPROACHES HIGH BACKED LEATHER CHAIR]*
Do you require an extra blanket, fruit; a book perhaps?

MORIARTY

A bible!

HOLMES

[LAUGHS HEARTILY] Gallows humour!

MORIARTY

Do you have a cigarette?

HOLMES

I have a Bradley.

MORIARTY

Too strong for my taste.

HOLMES

[SMILING] You have taste?

MORIARTY

Tut, tut.

HOLMES

I see a rather unpleasant winter ahead for you.

MORIARTY

Hope wins no battles! My will is that of stone.

HOLMES

How true. When I think of you, your skin is tinged with grey.

MORIARTY

That you think of me at all is - heartening.

HOLMES

You are but a distant shadow in my nightmares.

MORIARTY

I knew that they would take a hold of you.

HOLMES

Dear Moriarty, you are becoming feeble. As in fever, you grasp at passing words and images. You paint in the most lurid colours.

MORIARTY

Yes, and you are part of my landscape; do you not see? I see you as a simple child attempting to open a stout box containing the greatest conundrum. Try as you do, your attempts come to nought and the information contained therein remains a secret.

HOLMES

[UNCARING] How – abstract.

MORIARTY

Tell me detective, what secrets do you keep?

HOLMES

Secrets?

MORIARTY

Do not forget, my tentacles reach far and wide.

HOLMES

[DISGUSTED] Into the most debauched of places.

MORIARTY

I am able to assail once private rooms with ease.

HOLMES

I fear, [PLACES HIS FINGER TO HIS LIPS] I fear that confinement has addled your brain. Your words are the ramblings of a spent force. I see before me a husk of the man I once feared. I smell defeat. Now Moriarty, do your worst!

MORIARTY

'Worst'? I can only do what you see fit.

HOLMES

[EXASPERATED] See? Riddles! Give me straight talking or nothing!

HOLMES PACES. WITH A WAVE OF HIS HAND HE BECKONS MORIARTY TO SPEAK.

MORIARTY

It was never my intention to make an enemy of you but you *would* take on the mantle of busybody. We could have been allies.

HOLMES

[PIG SNORT] Allies? Ha!

MORIARTY

How unfortunate that you felt the need to play to the gallery. Sherlock Holmes – The Puritanical Detective.

HOLMES

[POINTS WITH MENACE] Hear this and take heed; my morals are stationed in the heavens whereas your heart and soul reside in the gutter. An alliance was never an option!

MORIARTY

You bastardise the words of Wilde to make good your point. I thought better of you – mistakenly it seems.

HOLMES

[INCENSED] Wilde? Do not tar me with the same brush as that *[QUIETLY]* deviant. He is a factory of unemotional quips. His raison d'être was to take away the breath and add a blush to the cheek of the undiscerning female. Do not, I say, do not cast me in the same role.

MORIARTY

[AFTER A BRIEF PAUSE] He betrayed his wife.

HOLMES

You are reduced to tittle tattle. This is common knowledge.

MORIARTY

For the love of a man.

HOLMES

That may be but it has no relevance within the framework of our conversation.

MORIARTY

You think not?

*HOLMES POINTS A FINGER IN THE DIRECTION OF THE HIGH BACKED
LEATHER CHAIR.*

HOLMES

Careful; you are entering that hinterland of conjecture and
speculation.

MORIARTY

My sentinels inform me that you were once presented with an
offer of warmth and affection from a female. I hear that it
was rebuked.

HOLMES

Tedious.

MORIARTY

And like Wilde, you found solace in the company of a man.

HOLMES

How irksome.

MORIARTY

We use the weapons that are available to us.

HOLMES

Your weapon of choice – at this juncture – is ineffectual.

MORIARTY

Think of it as my opening gambit.

*HOLMES TURNS HIS BACK TO THE CHAIR AND PLACES HIS HANDS BEHIND
HIS BACK.*

HOLMES

[SLY SMILE] Is this whole saga not – if I may borrow from
the French – a cliché? The pot calling the kettle black amuses
me. Let me remind you that when not at His Majesty's

pleasure you are to be found in the company of your youngest cohorts. All of whom, with the exception of the occasional runner, are male. I put it to you 'Mr' Moriarty; you should attend to your own beeswax.

MORIARTY

[CHUCKLING] That is the most entertainment I have had in many a long day. Thank you so much.

HOLMES

Your poison will soon be consigned to a dark room in history.

MORIARTY

Poison? I prefer to call it my powder which, by the by, I am keeping dry for the moment.

HOLMES

You may have a trick up your sleeve but it will serve you well to remember that your conspiracies will come to nought. It is over, Moriarty. Over!

SILENCE.

MORIARTY

So alike yet so different, are we not? *[SILENCE THEN]* Irene Adler!

HOLMES *RAISES HIS HAND TO COMMAND SILENCE.*

HOLMES

There is little point in raking over the past.

MORIARTY

Bested by 'the' woman.

HOLMES

[SNEERING] What would you know? I am all ears.

HOLMES *SITS CROSS LEGGED ON THE FLOOR.*

MORIARTY

Miriam. *[SILENCE THEN]* Her name was Miriam.
HOLMES
I see the wire of your snare.

MORIARTY
[PAINED] What would I know? Do you think that I came unto this earth fully formed, as you see me now? Do you think that the sun has never kissed my face? Do you think that I only elicit a smile when the spoils of battle lay at my feet? How little you know. How little you know of me.

HOLMES
[QUIETLY] Miriam? A conquest?

MORIARTY
A wife.

HOLMES
[UNIMPRESSED] A wife. *[BORED SIGH]*

MORIARTY
Is such a thing beyond the realms of possibility?

HOLMES
[YAWNING] Perhaps I should take a seat if this is to be a protracted affair.

MORIARTY
I think that you should; you show signs of fatigue.

HOLMES
[TETCHILY] Enough! Your story if you please.

MORIARTY
Very well. At nineteen years of age I decided to take a break from my studies and visit a family member – a brother – at his smallholding in the north. It was a blessed relief to vacate my damp lodgings.

HOLMES
[PATRONISING] And you deduced that the country air would

revive you. Capital! This brother; may I be permitted to ask his name?

MORIARTY

James.

HOLMES

[AS IF MAKING NOTE IN A BOOK] Thank you. *[SMILES]* Please continue. 'A smallholding in the north.'

MORIARTY

My brother and his wife constantly skirted along the edges of penury but although a lack of pennies limited their expenditure it did not curtail their happiness.

HOLMES

This has more than a whiff of red herring about it but I am willing to play along – for now.

MORIARTY

I spent eight idyllic weeks with them helping out wherever I could. I found it pleasing to turn my hand to simple chores such as chopping wood for the fire, repairing fences and resettling roof slates. I would have willingly done more but unfortunately my skills were limited.

HOLMES

How very rural. So, please furnish me with the details in which you met your grand amour.

MORIARTY

It was accidental – design had no part to play in the introduction.

HOLMES

Continue.

MORIARTY

In my guise as collector of firewood I stumbled upon the rotting remains of a felled oak close to the brook. I was alone, or so I thought, when I heard a cry for assistance. I advanced.

HOLMES

[SICKLY SMILE] This was Miriam?

MORIARTY

Yes.

HOLMES

And of course upon seeing her your heart raced, etc, etc.
[WITH A SENSE OF URGENCY] Do carry on.

MORIARTY

She nursed a small spaniel dog in her arms. Her tears, I
observed, perhaps inappropriately considering the
circumstances, glistened in the morning sunlight. My
approach appeared to be most welcome. 'Sir,' she sobbed,
'you have arrived at a most salient moment for Boot, my dog,
that which I love more than anything else in this world, has
suffered an injury. His paw has been skewered by a thorn
from a nearby bramble bush.' My knowledge of animals was
scant at best as I had little contact with more than a stray
feline or watched as a horse pulled a cart. Still, I was adamant
that I would be of service. I knelt beside her without words.
Taking the animal's paw I observed said thorn. It had pierced
the skin and a small amount of blood was in evidence.
'Please avert your gaze for a moment.' She complied. A short
yelp and the thorn was removed. 'There. I suggest that you
bathe the wound upon your return home.' Another stream of
tears was followed by her profuse thanks and good wishes.

HOLMES

[EXHALING] You place yourself in the role of Androlcles.
How charming. Your vocation, it appears, seems to have
evaded you – Aesop. Pray – continue.

MORIARTY

A most illuminating tale unfolded as I escorted her –

HOLMES

In her hour of need –

19

MORIARTY

- as I escorted her home, canine in my arms.

HOLMES

And this illuminating tale?

MORIARTY

Her grandparents, Philippe and Miriam Dupont, of French and Portuguese extraction, fled the Bastille on that final day of liberation having escaped the blade of Madame Guillotine. With France on its knees and close to buckling, Philippe, along with his wife, made for England with all haste. They settled in the north and bore a single child; Mathilde. On her eighteenth birthday she married the local squire; Jacob Barton, with the proviso that that name of Dupont would live on. As Barton's love for Mathilde was great he saw to it that his wife would bear the hyphen Dupont-Barton. Jacob and Mathilde gave issue to Miriam.

HOLMES

[BORED] And so on, and so on. I take it that - *[SARCASTICALLY]* please forgive me for truncating what is truly a most fascinating tale – you married this Miriam Dupont-Barton and lived happily - ?

MORIARTY

[POIGNANTLY] Happily? Happiness can be bittersweet and short lived. We too, had issue.

HOLMES

[WITH A CHILL] Another Moriarty?

MORIARTY

Twins – sons.

HOLMES

And what has become of your 'issue?'

MORIARTY

Alas, a fever took hold, my wife was not spared.*[TEARFUL]*

It seemed to last for an eternity and – *[SPRIGHTLY]* and here we are!

HOLMES

Your story is truly magnificent. *[CLAPPING HIS HANDS]* Oh, well done, bravo! I congratulate you. *[LAUGHS HEARTILY]* It has been many a long day since I stood witness to such an amusing tale. No doubt the spirits of Messrs Dickens and Poe are in turmoil knowing that the pen of James Moriarty is weaving such delightfully lurid tales. Forgive my laughter *[COMPOSES HIMSELF]* I must restrain myself.

MORIARTY

You found my story interesting?

HOLMES

My interest does not make it interesting.

MORIARTY

You are impenetrable, Sherlock Holmes; you are as a clam.

HOLMES

Neither a clam nor a fool. Why bare your soul to me; your mortal enemy?

MORIARTY

You allowed me to. I told you of things that no living man has heard before.

HOLMES

I prefer you to talk, otherwise I will suspect you of plotting.

MORIARTY

Why, in these circumstances do you not lower your portcullis? We are but two men away from the distractions of the outside world; answerable to none but ourselves. If I ask you to break bread with me you will curl your lip at my offer? If I ask you to smoke a bowl you will suspect a secreted hallucinogenic. Tell me Sherlock Holmes, what shaped you so?

HOLMES

[UNCONCERNED] Have you finished? [SMILES] Tell me –
[TAKES A DIAMOND FROM HIS POCKET AND PLACES
IT INTO THE PALM OF HIS HAND] I was wondering if you
would be so kind as to appraise this most delicate of stones
for me.

MORIARTY

It shines – it sparkles – it is a diamond.

HOLMES

What a shame; I was expecting a much more detailed
analysis from the person purporting to be none other than
John Robert Bellman. I am obviously wasting my time here.

MORIARTY

Ha! Do you think you have unriddled me Sherlock Holmes?
Did you really think I would make it so easy without reason?

HOLMES

Regardless, I have most certainly found you out.

MORIARTY

I assure you, no applause will be forthcoming.

HOLMES

You advertised heavily upon your arrest. That such a ruffian
made public his dissatisfaction at being apprehended alarmed
me much – especially as Bellman, to my certain knowledge,
sleeps in a watery grave close to Teignmouth, if my sources
are to be believed.

MORIARTY

By 'sources', I take it that you refer to your 'children.' Your
irregulars.

HOLMES

Dear me, no. The irregulars so far south? That would never
do. My information came by way of a keen eyed young
police constable destined for greater things; but I digress –

MORIARTY

You are a highly tuned individual, Sherlock Holmes.

HOLMES

[PAINED LOOK] Am I?

MORIARTY

Come; sit! In the little time afforded us perhaps we should compare notes?

HOLMES

Without hindrance?

MORIARTY

Without hindrance indeed. We are older now and our past should remain so. I would find an exchange of information preferable to our Swiss adventure.

HOLMES

Which, to this day, remains a secret.

MORIARTY

What would I stand to gain by having the truth made public? You threw in with me then; albeit with the strongest reservations, but still –

HOLMES

It was mutual.

MORIARTY

The only time that we colluded. Please sit.

HOLMES SITS IN THE HIGH BACKED LEATHER CHAIR. DRAWS HIS KNEES UP TO HIS CHIN.

HOLMES

I demand full and frank disclosure.

MORIARTY

As do I.

HOLMES

There is much I need to know and I will tolerate only – only the truth!

MORIARTY

Then let us begin.

HOLMES

Very well. *[**HOLMES** RUBS HIS HANDS TOGETHER EAGERLY]*

MORIARTY

I must warn you 'detective' that should the information that I am about to impart find its way to the authorities then things will go bad for you. I am loyal to my family. My words are for your ears alone.

HOLMES

We are wasting time! Cast your 'mind' back to 1897.

MORIARTY

A vintage year for crime I seem to recall.

HOLMES

Then you no doubt recollect the affair at Versailles?

MORIARTY

Ah, The Blackbird.

HOLMES

Yes, Don Leonardo Merlo in his guise as The Blackbird of Milan. The missing Botticelli; did it find its way into your hands?

MORIARTY

I am afraid not.

HOLMES

Merlo was never in your employ?

MORIARTY

That is not what I said.

HOLMES

[EXASPERATED] Oh, please! This is insufferable!

MORIARTY

The Austrian oils.

HOLMES

[EXCITEDLY] Yes? What do you know of them?

MORIARTY

Don Leonardo was most certainly responsible and yes; they found their way to my table.

HOLMES

That is impossible! At that point he was dead. I accompanied Watson to the autopsy.

MORIARTY

Are you certain it was who you thought it to be? Wanted it to be? Things are not always as they appear to be, as you know well. You certainly attended the examination but I could not tell you who was laying on that cold marble slab as I am not privy to that information.

HOLMES

Tell me –

MORIARTY

Let me save you mental anguish; The Blackbird lives.

HOLMES

I calculate that he is 80 years of age.

MORIARTY

And as nimble fingered as ever. And now –

HOLMES

I await your instruction.

MORIARTY

It will not have escaped your attention that my recent activities have been seriously curtailed - age transcends the most meticulous plotting and planning – and it has fallen to my generals to do much of the field work.

HOLMES

Little change.

MORIARTY

[IMPATIENTLY] If you would be so kind.

HOLMES

[SNEERING] Please, do carry on.

MORIARTY

A certain member of my flock by the name of Wakefield, brother of the late Reverend Horatio Wakefield, who I believe served with your doctor in the Afghan conflict –

HOLMES

Watson tells me how his words were of comfort to him when a stray bullet laid him low.

MORIARTY

[TERSE] No illumination! A simple answer to a simple question if you please! Were you responsible for his incarceration?

HOLMES

There was damning proof of his involvement in at least three major crimes in the Whitechapel district alone.

MORIARTY

And upon his arrest *[FAGIN-ISH]* was he carrying anything about his person?

HOLMES

Such as?

MORIARTY

[ANGRILY] Please do not make me work for my supper, Sherlock Holmes, for restraints or no, I will –

HOLMES

Dear 'Professor,' my procrastination was justified. Your impatience tells me that the documents he had secreted about his person were of issue to you.

MORIARTY

[SHARP INTAKE OF BREATH] They belong to me!

HOLMES

Then perhaps you should caper along to Bow Street and retrieve them.

MORIARTY

You have not yet unravelled the ciphers.

HOLMES

Time has not been kind. I will assign a late evening to them.

MORIARTY

As you wish but they could prove to be your undoing.

HOLMES

To trade these titbits has been most - pleasing – but my time is at a premium and I must take my leave of you.

MORIARTY

[FEIGNING DISMAY] Oh dear and we were getting along so well.

HOLMES

Be that as it may –

MORIARTY

I have kept back my highest card until last.

HOLMES

[EXASPERATED] Will you give readily or must I eke it out, inch by inch?

MORIARTY

Are you a betting man, Sherlock Holmes?

HOLMES

I prefer certainties.

MORIARTY

What price would you give me on exiting this place before you?

HOLMES

Ha!

MORIARTY

Dwell a moment or two; afford me this luxury.

HOLMES

You will gain little by reminiscing now.

MORIARTY

Perhaps.

HOLMES

You have something to say? No tittle tattle.

MORIARTY

That day; that first meeting in your rooms.

HOLMES

Detail!

MORIARTY

Certain liberties were taken in print. Your 'Doctor' chronicles you in a favourable light yet he paints a likeness of me that is most unflattering – most unbecoming.

HOLMES

Is this by way of a complaint?

MORIARTY

It is by way of the truth.

HOLMES

A commodity that has evaded you thus far.

MORIARTY

I have document of that, our first meeting, and if you are as you say you are, a straight talker, you will see it as a true account. Allow me to read. The day augured well; I had taken breakfast and made my way to your rooms in Baker Street, as instructed, a little after 10 am. I was ushered in by the Belle of Inverness.

HOLMES

The Belle of Inverness?

MORIARTY

Later! You paced impatiently like a hot tempered child. "I appear to be a trifle late," I said consulting my timepiece. You bade me to sit without greeting. I was ill at ease as you constantly toyed with a one shot pistol. I felt as a schoolboy summoned to his master's study. Although this was our first face to face encounter I felt I knew you well. You insisted that the bartering commenced instantly, curtailing any possible pleasantries. You looked deep into my face; drinking in every line.

HOLMES

"You are a much older man than I imagined."

MORIARTY

"There is little that I can change there." Once again you fingered the pistol that lay beside you and the threat to my person hung heavily.

HOLMES

"I have underlined the problems that perturb me."

MORIARTY

You read from a pocket book in which you had scribbled down some salient points.

HOLMES

"You crossed my path on the 4th of January. On the 23rd you incommoded me. By the middle of February I was seriously inconvenienced by you. The situation is becoming an impossible one."

MORIARTY

"Untenable, perhaps, not impossible."

HOLMES

"You must cease your activities. You must withdraw."

MORIARTY

"And if I refuse?"

HOLMES

"Then it will go bad for you."

MORIARTY

"Danger is part of our trade is it not?"

HOLMES

"Then look upon my threat as inevitable destruction!"

MORIARTY

"If there is nothing else then I will take my leave of you; I have business elsewhere."

HOLMES

"Should our paths cross again - they assuredly will - I will find a solution that pleases me."

MORIARTY

"Think long and hard on 'solutions' Mr. Sherlock Holmes, but with a clear head that is not addled by enhancements."

HOLMES

A vivid retelling of the truth.

MORIARTY

You know that within your 'heart' they are cold facts.

HOLMES

[HOLDING BOTH HANDS TO HIS EARS] I am deaf to your protestations.

MORIARTY

Why do I waste my breath?

HOLMES

That will be short lived.

MORIARTY

I have much to live for. I have a business to run. I have built an empire from dust.

HOLMES

Dust to dust.

MORIARTY

You are aware that my employees hold me in high esteem.

HOLMES

[UNIMPRESSED] How nice. Such thoughts would have kept you warm in your dotage but alas, the hangman calls.

MORIARTY

I hear that they have labelled me the Napoleon of crime?

HOLMES

'Branded' you! *[SNIFFS HAUGHTILY]* You may well find that it was I who originated that phrase and now they use it to flatter you. It is commonplace for a dog to lick the boots of a cruel master.

MORIARTY

That may be, but you bestow upon me such a title and yet you do not – will not – yield to my superiority.

HOLMES

Superiority? Ha! Your fall, when it comes – and mark my words it will – your fall will show you to be the charlatan that I always knew you to be. I will relish the moment. It will be – delicious!

MORIARTY

Leave!

HOLMES

As you wish.

HOLMES CROSSES TO THE DOOR. MAKES TO TURN THE HANDLE THEN STOPS. HE TURNS BACK. FACES THE AUDIENCE.

MORIARTY

What troubles you?

HOLMES

If I may be permitted one final indulgence.

MORIARTY

[EVIL CHUCKLE] But of course.

HOLMES

I have pondered and theorised and drawn a blank.

MORIARTY

Your question!

HOLMES

Your name.

MORIARTY

My name? My, my, detective; perhaps it is time that you found gainful employment.

HOLMES

James Moriarty. Are you a hyphen or a bar sinister? That is the conundrum. You cite that you lodged with a brother of that very name – James! I know it to be fact that you too hold that prefix. Two members of the same family - two brothers, no less - sharing a first name? What are you hiding? A shame? A sack of bones in the Moriarty family wardrobe?

MORIARTY
[WITH MENACE] Back down Sherlock Holmes!

HOLMES
[TRIUMPHANTLY] Ha! Perhaps I have 'unriddled' you after all.

MORIARTY
Be on your guard, Jeremy.

HOLMES
Dear Moriarty, you grasp at thin air. There is a natural order to these things and no matter how you scream and flail the inevitable will come to pass. This is a most satisfactory solution to our many years of jousting. I will mark the occasion of your drop by raising a glass and toasting the end of plague and menace. Far too many times have you evaded me, far too many times have you shown me a clean pair of heels but this is the end of you, 'Mr. Moriarty.' I must go. This air is far too thick for my constitution.

MORIARTY
Please forgive me Sherlock Holmes. You see before you a beaten man. I bow to your winning hand.

HOLMES
Your words will not sway the inevitable outcome so cast all thoughts of leniency to one side.

MORIARTY
I concur and will take my punishment, but as you see I am past my best and infirm. I am belittled. I no longer have the ability to fasten my own boot laces. That a man who once sent shivers throughout the known world should be reduced to this canker you see before you is the final humiliation. Look upon me with mercy, Sherlock Holmes. *[PITIFUL]* Please?

HOLMES

It would not do to have you trip on your way to the gallows.

*HOLMES KNEELS BEFORE **MORIARTY** IN ORDER TO TIE HIS BOOT LACES.*

MORIARTY

How fitting that you should kneel before me. Now, let us see
how you fare against cayenne! *[**HOLMES** RECOILS
MOMENTARILY BLINDED. HE RUBS VICIOUSLY AT HIS
EYES]* I knew that you would be susceptible to my plea,
much more than you are to your seven percent solution!

*HOLMES DARTS TO THE BED AND RETRIEVES HIS WALKING CANE FROM
WHICH HE PRODUCES A FENCING FOIL. HOLDS FOIL IN LEFT HAND THEN
SWAPS TO RIGHT. [**JEREMY BRETT** WAS LEFT HANDED] HE SWIPES IN
MORIARTY'S DIRECTION.*

HOLMES

The solution, dear Moriarty, is in my hands. What is your
preference? Sabre or foil - or do you have a persuader
concealed about your person?

MORIARTY

When I cut you deep dear Jeremy please do not cry. A man
should never shed tears.

*HOLMES BACKS AWAY FROM THE HIGH BACKED LEATHER CHAIR AS IF
PURSUED. HE JUMPS ONTO THE BED AND SWISHES HIS BLADE BACK AND
FORTH. A GLANCE TOWARDS THE DOOR IS FOLLOWED BY A LEAP TOWARDS
IT. HE STUMBLES AND HIS FOIL FALLS TO THE FLOOR. BY WAY OF
PROTECTION HE RAISES HIS RIGHT HAND IN FRONT OF HIS FACE. IT IS CUT.
HE HOLDS IT WITH HIS LEFT HAND. BLOOD FLOWS. THE PAIN IS EVIDENT
FROM THE GRIMACE ON HIS FACE.*

DORAN

[OFF] And in the meantime if there's anything I can get for
you let me know.

*HOLMES CRAWLS WEAKLY TO THE CENTRE OF THE ROOM. HE APPEARS
DAZED.*

MORIARTY

It is over now Sherlock Holmes. Rest well. I will take my leave of you forever as I set sail to a new world, a new life, a new alias.

HOLMES

But you are Moriarty.

MORIARTY

Am I?

DORAN

[OFF] These rooms are a little sparse.

MORIARTY

Ha, ha, ha, ha, ha, ha, ha!

HOLMES IS LYING FACE DOWN ON THE FLOOR. HIS LEFT HAND RESTS BENEATH HIS HEAD. HIS RIGHT ARM IS STRETCHED OUT BEFORE HIM. HE APPEARS LIFELESS.

WATSON

[CALLING] Holmes?

HOLMES

[REMAINS MOTIONLESS. HIS REPLY IS STRAINED]
Watson?

WATSON

[FRAUGHT] I came as soon as I – *[TAKEN ABACK]* What abnormality is this?

HOLMES

[IN A STUPOR. CALLS OUT WEAKLY] Watson? Is it really you?

GROANS. RAISES HIS RIGHT HAND ABOVE HIS HEAD AND POINTS TO THE HEAVENS. MAKES A FIST IN TRIUMPH.

My Watson!

WATSON

Holmes, what on earth has happened? Here, let me help you. Soon have you back on your feet old boy.

HOLMES LIFTS HIMSELF GINGERLY TO HIS FEET. APPEARS FEEBLE AS HE COLLAPSES ONTO THE BED.

HOLMES

Still the same caring Watson.

WATSON

Of course! I rushed here as soon as I received the telegram from Falkner.

HOLMES

[BLANK] Falkner?

WATSON

It's not like you to forget a name, Holmes?

HOLMES

[TROUBLED] Forgive me my friend but my mind is in a fog. Please go on.

WATSON

Well, when we vacated these rooms, Mrs. Hudson, by way of retiring, sold the property to a young chemist by the name of Falkner. He is a reputable fellow and is building quite a reputation for himself. His name is spoken of in glowing terms.

HOLMES

[PONDERING] Falkner?

WATSON

You seem perplexed old boy?

HOLMES

I was ruminating on how I came to be here, back in our old haunt.

WATSON

I can't say I am entirely sure of the details. Falkner said you almost removed the paint from the door, banging with your fists. You demanded he afford you entrance.

HOLMES

[A LOOK OF CONCERN] And yet, I have no recollection of the incident whatsoever.

WATSON

He went on to say that he saw the state of high anxiety that you were in and was compassionate enough to accommodate you, letting you rest on his sofa where I find you now.

HOLMES

[UNMOVED] How gracious of Mr. Falkner.

WATSON

Yes.

HOLMES

And – where – is Mrs. Hudson?

WATSON

Ah, sadly, she died, almost two years ago. It was that abominable winter.

HOLMES

[EMOTIONLESS] How sad.

WATSON

And you have no recollection of any of this?

HOLMES

Annoyingly not! *[PATS HIS POCKETS AS IF SEARCHING FOR SOMETHING. STOPS]* Watson, would you be kind enough to tell me the time? Please!

WATSON

Why, it is close on 7.45.

HOLMES

[RUNS A FINGER LIGHTLY ACROSS HIS BROW] And the day?

WATSON

The day?

HOLMES

Amuse me. Be kind enough to tell me the day and the date.

WATSON

[BEMUSED] It is Wednesday, the 10th of April, 1912.

HOLMES, DEEP IN THOUGHT PLACES BOTH HIS HANDS OVER HIS MOUTH.

HOLMES

I see.

WATSON

[ALARMED] Holmes! Your hand!

HOLMES

[WAVES THE PROBLEM AWAY WITH A FLOURISH] Stay yourself dear doctor! It is a trifle and nothing more.

WATSON

You must allow me to dress it!

HOLMES

I assure you that a bandage would 'reek' of the melodramatic. It is a scratch at best.

WATSON

Then you must tell me how it came to be.

HOLMES

Ha!

WATSON

You laugh but I can see from the severity of your wound that there is no comical story attached to it.

HOLMES

You misconstrued my ejaculation! *[Calmly]* I am in good company and for the moment that is all that matters.

WATSON

Jolly nice of you to say so Holmes. I am heartened to see you, especially in these surroundings; the rooms in which we shared many of our triumphs.

HOLMES

Dear Watson, I sense that you are but a sentence away from waxing lyrical and revisiting past adventures.

WATSON

Well, it happens that - *[HOLMES RAISES HIS HAND BY WAY OF ORDERING WATSON TO STOP]* only two days ago – what is it?

HOLMES

My mouth is dry.

WATSON

It may be the after effects of shock?

HOLMES

Quite possibly. This event has left me thirsting for one of Mrs. Hudson's delicious cups of tea but alas –

WATSON

I could go and have a word with Falkner's man. He is an amiable fellow and I am sure that to serve tea to England's pre-eminent detective –

HOLMES

Private consulting detective!

WATSON

Ha! Regardless of title, I am sure that he would be honoured to prepare a cup of Lapsang Souchong for the celebrated Sherlock Holmes!

HOLMES

[STIFLING A SMILE] You are far too kind.

WATSON

But you still have some much needed explaining to do.

HOLMES

All in good time my dear fellow. *[STRETCHING]* How have I survived for so long without you at my side?

WATSON

But you have reported regularly that all is well with you in Sussex. Do you lack stimulation? Do you have a sounding board there?

HOLMES

[DRYLY] Only Mathilde.

WATSON

[CHUCKLING] Mathilde? Oh yes? Pray tell!

HOLMES

[SHARP BREATH] Your broad grin suggests cheap tittle tattle and a lurid romantic interlude; let me provide you with some necessary data –

WATSON

[EAGERLY] Please go on.

HOLMES

Mathilde is a Queen –

WATSON

[AGOG] Royalty!

HOLMES

[Exasperated] A Queen bee.

WATSON

[AFTER SEVERAL SECONDS. DISMAYED] A bee?

HOLMES

[HAUGHTILY] A Queen bee, Watson, and as such should be afforded the privileges of any sovereign!

WATSON

[DUMBFOUNDED] But a bee?

HOLMES

I see dissatisfaction and disappointment etched upon your face. It is at odds with the colouration of your skin brought about by too much sun whilst fishing in the Lake District.

WATSON

[AMUSED] Ha! Still the same old Holmes! Now what can it be? What was it that gave away that information? Was it mud on my boots indigenous to the region or something else?

HOLMES

Simply a casual observation and nothing more. Even a blind man could see that you cut short your holiday and travelled back to London on the 11.35 from Workington.

WATSON

I'll be blowed if I can fathom how you arrived at that conclusion.

HOLMES

But the correct one – yes?

WATSON

Yes. Please explain?

HOLMES

[EXHALING] Oh dear, so trivial. *[MATTER OF FACTLY]* You inadvertently left a fishing fly in the lapel of your tweed, the bottom of your trousers appear crumpled, suggesting that they have been tucked into your socks – you tend to do this when fishing from a river bank.

WATSON

And the time?

HOLMES

[A CHUCKLE] Here I cheated. Your used ticket stub is peeking from your waistcoat pocket. That observation I put down to your toilette and not my deductive powers. So you see, casual observation!

WATSON

I can say quite categorically that you are still as sharp as a pin!

HOLMES

[SARCASTICALLY] Such an accolade.

WATSON

Tea?

HOLMES

[DISMISSIVELY] It matters not.

WATSON

It would be no trouble.

HOLMES

[DOMINANTLY] Please sit down.

WATSON

Are you yet able to formulate how you came to be here in Baker Street?

HOLMES

Alas not. I do, however, have a series of theories that I would like to put to the test if you would be so kind?

WATSON

I would be delighted. Should I take notes?

HOLMES

As you so wish.

WATSON

It's quite like old times.

HOLMES

[DISMAYED] Please!

WATSON

Sorry. I am ready.

HOLMES

My facts may be fragmented due to the clouded circumstances that brought me to be here but I have managed to retain the salient points. They are as follows; I am sure that you have been keeping abreast of the recent spate of 'garottings' in the county of Gloucestershire?

WATSON

[HESITANTLY] Unfortunately not.

HOLMES

Then the name Lampton will be of no import to you?

WATSON

[LIGHT BULB MOMENT] Hold on! The Sixways Strangler!

HOLMES

The Sixways Strangler indeed! Good old Watson.

WATSON

His name was mentioned in The Lancet only last month.

HOLMES

Then you know of his methods?

HOLMES

Yes. The report stated how a left handed man – friend Lampton – had devised an ingenious method of damaging the cervical vertebrae with his right hand. This way he was able to step out of the shadow of suspicion after carrying out his grisly deeds.

HOLMES

Ha! But no longer!

WATSON

I hear he stews in Newgate while awaiting trail.

HOLMES

Yes, I know.

WATSON

It was you?

HOLMES

Via a telegram to Scotland Yard.

WATSON

May I ask what alerted you to him?

HOLMES

In my guise of street arab I was able to lubricate Larkin, his cohort, who has the loosest of tongues when inebriated.

WATSON

Who by all accounts has the charm of a snake? Was he not discovered attempting to sell the church bells of his local parish without the clergy's knowledge?

HOLMES

Please Watson; you know that I have a high disregard for church bells, especially when they peel The Nine Tailors, since our encounter with Stockdale, the Chesterfield cannibal.

WATSON

Stockdale! That case is still confined to my notebook, The Adventure of The Devil's Spire.

HOLMES

[CRESTFALLEN] The Devil's Spire indeed! You have a flair for the outrageous. That case, even after our deaths, must remain locked in the vault of Cox and Company of Charing Cross. You have already given me your word on that matter.

WATSON

And I would never betray a confidence.

HOLMES

I know that you are the most honourable of men Watson, and I do not bestow accolades lightly. I cannot foresee a time when the public would be ready for such a diabolical tale.

WATSON

So, in stating that you befriended Larkin in one of your numerous disguises, it tells me that you have indeed been back in harness?

HOLMES

[SOMBRE] A necessity borne out by the fact that we face a terror with far reaching consequences.

WATSON

Sounds grave?

HOLMES

Indeed.

WATSON

And Lampton is at the centre of it.

HOLMES

Not the centre Watson, he is very much on the periphery, a foot soldier. We need to find the pea beneath the thimble for what is about to unfold is sleight of hand on a grand scale. Allow me to drop two more names into the pot, the first of which is Cavendish –

WATSON

[ASTONISHED] Major George Cavendish?

HOLMES

So, a Major now? I swear his rank changes like the seasons.

WATSON

[DAZED] Major George Cavendish.

HOLMES

A bitter pill?

WATSON

But he moves in such exalted circles?

HOLMES

[UNIMPRESSED] Does he really?

WATSON

And what of his sister Judith and her charitable works?

HOLMES

[MOCKING] Sister? His concubine! *[MATTER OF FACTLY]*
By the by, her given name is Maude. Her true surname is still
a mystery to all.

WATSON

But she is knocking on the door of royalty?

HOLMES

[DISPARAGINGLY] Royalty? I warn you, do not be taken in
by her feminine wiles!

WATSON

I was simply repeating what is public knowledge.

HOLMES

Does this 'public knowledge' dot the i's and cross the t's of
the Pendry case?

WATSON

Surely not?

HOLMES

Oh yes. It was Maude Cavendish - I call her Cavendish so
that your notes will have a point of reference - it was Maude
Cavendish who despatched him.

WATSON

[TAKEN ABACK] How could a woman commit such a
dreadful act?

HOLMES

[DEVILISHLY] Fear not dear doctor, I am told that the sea is plentiful. [TAKES SEVERAL PACES ACROSS THE ROOM. COMES TO A HALT AND RAISES A FINGER] And now to one of the lowest blackguards it has been my misfortune to look upon; Bellman!

WATSON

[DRAWING BREATH] The assassin!

HOLMES

I see by your sharp intake that this fiend is known to you?

WATSON

"A formidable force not to be taken lightly." So said The Telegraph in the wake of recent events on the Continent.

HOLMES

And now he is billeted here, in London. My sources tell me that he is sharpening his claws in Beak Street.

WATSON

If you know this then why is he still at liberty?

HOLMES

Watson, Watson, Watson; to apprehend him now would be folly. We will wait – and watch – and when the time is right [MAKES A FIST] we will swoop! At present he is cloaked by a force so strong that I fear he is beyond the reach of the authorities.

WATSON

Are you admitting defeat?

HOLMES

There are times when probability far outweighs possibility. I cannot enter into this lightly. The odds are stacked against us.

WATSON

But we have faced formidable odds in the past and

triumphed. Surely these three villains can be brought down?

HOLMES

Ordinarily, the triumvirate of Lampton, Cavendish and Bellman I would see as ineffectual and it would not cause me a moment's unease, but the glue that has bound them together is a different prospect entirely.

WATSON

I fear you are keeping the heart of the matter away from me Holmes.

HOLMES

And with good reason.

WATSON

[CONCERNED] Holmes?

HOLMES

[APPROACHING SADNESS] I fear that my words will test the bounds of our friendship and –

WATSON

What is it?

HOLMES

Our friendship is all I have ever been able to rely upon.

WATSON

You know that nothing you say could shake me. We have endured so much over these long years and been in many tight scrapes. Please lay your case before me.

HOLMES

There are certain details that I kept from you for your safety.

WATSON

Go on?

HOLMES

Certain details pertaining to *[CLOSES HIS EYES]* the despicable Professor Moriarty.

WATSON

[SHOCKED] Moriarty?

HOLMES

The embodiment of evil!

WATSON

But I thought we had heard the last of him? So many years have passed without mention of his name.

HOLMES

[WITH BRAVADO] His name? *[RAPIDLY] His* name still causes me great consternation and his withered hand is but a fingertip away at all times. I am capable of withstanding the sternest mental opposition - you can vouch for this, Watson - but *he*, after these many years, is still able to defile my thoughts.

WATSON

Can you not see that your words border on obsession? He can harm you no more.

HOLMES

Ha! *[SPAT]* Your words are based on a lack of necessary data.

WATSON

Then perhaps you can illuminate me?

HOLMES

I fear I made the costliest of decisions when my defences were momentarily breached.

WATSON

You must explain.

*SILENCE. **HOLMES** WRAPS HIMSELF IN HIS ARMS. HE HANGS HIS HEAD.*

HOLMES

I fear the words will not come.

WATSON

You must tell me!

HOLMES

Then I must first draw your attention to that last day at Reichenbach.

WATSON

Reichenbach? How could I ever forget? I recall it vividly for a multitude of reasons and in particular your encounter with Moriarty. How I wish that I could have taken my place alongside you.

HOLMES

Our meeting was no chance affair.

WATSON

Arranged?

HOLMES

Please Watson, if you will afford me five minutes uninterrupted then I will reveal – the truth.

WATSON

I feel you owe me that much.

HOLMES

[AWAITING SILENCE] If you would be so kind?

WATSON

Please continue.

SFX

WATERFALL

HOLMES

That day still plagues me. I was given strict instructions that I must meet Moriarty alone. You may recall the note you received as we headed towards the summit; manufactured in order to have you return to our hotel in the valley below. A simple piece of theatre; a medical emergency. A coronary if I recall?

WATSON

A haemorrhage!

HOLMES

[PLACES FINGER TO LIP] It was the work of a moment. The note was intended to send you scurrying back to aid a fictitious patient. Moriarty's confederates – for there was more than one – had devised a way to remove you from the final act, thus allowing their leader to show his hand. I clambered towards the mouth of the river, as arranged, and there he was; a frail, determined sack of dry bones. I could have snuffed out his life, much like a cockroach under the sole of my boot had I so wished.

WATSON

But for some inexplicable reason you chose not to?

HOLMES

[ANGRILY] I am not in the business of granting absolution nor snatching mortality away from those who have wronged me!

WATSON

If you wish to know how I feel; you afforded that parasite unwarranted respect.

HOLMES

I did not ask for an opinion.

WATSON

That is unwarranted!

HOLMES

[TERSE] If I may continue? I observed that he had arrived ahead of time to afford composure; his breathing was regular, for a man of his years, and his manner relaxed. Though I was aware his senses were alerted to my presence, he neither

flinched nor acknowledged my arrival. I approached cautiously but his raised hand bade me to halt.

MORIARTY

"Sherlock Holmes. Have you come to peddle your wares?"

HOLMES

"Sir!"

MORIARTY

"You will not afford me my name?"

HOLMES

"You have so many to play with."

MORIARTY

"Tut, tut."

HOLMES

He beckoned me with a long un-manicured finger. My nerve ends tingled but it was paramount that I follow instruction. It was clear that he had already picked out a spot for our meeting. I perched alongside him. We sat, no more than an arm's length from each other, looking out in opposite directions over the Lauterbrunnen Valley as the unharnessed power of the Reichenbach roared below.

MORIARTY

"I was sure that you would come."

HOLMES

"How so?"

MORIARTY

"Your curiosity, dear Holmes -"

HOLMES

"Dear Holmes"? "What a fascinating glimpse you afford me into your psyche."

MORIARTY

[MOCKING TONE] "Did I slip? Tread carefully here as the risks are high."

HOLMES

His tone belied the danger at hand.

MORIARTY

"This is a mean spirited reunion."

HOLMES

I could not afford to drop my guard for a second.

MORIARTY

"We find ourselves in something of a pickle?"

HOLMES

"I am afraid that I can not trivialise what has passed between us."

MORIARTY

"Nor I but we must view our past encounters as minor skirmishes. We have bigger fish to fry do we not?"

HOLMES

"So, what is it to be? I have been remiss and failed to bring a firearm so a duel is out of the question? A fist fight?"

MORIARTY

"I fear your flair for the melodramatic rears its head; besides, you have youth and agility in your favour. Two men of intellect in a fist fight? I think not! How undignified!"

HOLMES

"Dignity appears to have eluded you thus far, for you have behaved in the most reprehensible manner to date."

MORIARTY

"Your behavioural analysis has no bearing on the matter in hand. I say this; you must revise your plans to best me. We must start again anew, for the good of all parties."

HOLMES

"Hoc finis est."

MORIARTY

"Precisely! I see little point in snuffing out each other's candles in what amounts to childish folly."

HOLMES

"Be so kind as to let me hear your proposal."

MORIARTY

"It is simply this; you must curb your activities and be blind to me for a period of – should we say – five years – possibly three? After such time, you may go about your everyday 'business."

HOLMES

"The feeling of déjà vu is insurmountable."

MORIARTY

"Our meeting - albeit a brief one – in your rooms was *toute autre chose*. My bargaining powers were not at a premium then."

HOLMES

[Smug smile] "And what do you have in your armoury now that could possibly force my hand?"

MORIARTY

"I have life – human life!"

HOLMES

I must admit that my blood, such as it was, ran to a chill. I was defenceless.

WATSON

Sorry Holmes but I must interject - human life?

HOLMES

[SIGH] I thought that by adopting my methods you would

have arrived at the only conclusion possible. The life, my dear Watson, was yours. You have always been of supreme importance to me.

WATSON

[EXHALING HEAVILY] My life?

HOLMES

[CLAPS HIS HANDS TOGETHER AND SMILES] But here you are! I made certain that no harm would befall my dear friend regardless of consequence.

WATSON

My intuition tells me that what followed was compromise?

HOLMES

You have a propensity to fall back on intuition when logic is called for. *[HEAVY SIGH]* A compromise indeed! Now, if I may be permitted to continue?

WATSON

Of course.

HOLMES

I was cornered. I felt the hiss of the cobra upon my neck.

MORIARTY

"So, what say you, Mr. Sherlock Holmes? Do you agree to cease trading for such a period?"

HOLMES

"You have left me little room to manoeuvre."

MORIARTY

"But all is fair in love and war?"

HOLMES

[ANGERED] "Fair?"

MORIARTY

"The angles compute do they not?"

HOLMES

"If I am to allow you this liberty then there must be at least one proviso in my favour."

MORIARTY

"Let me hear it. I will see if I can accommodate?"

HOLMES

"What of your underlings?"

MORIARTY

"Do with them what you will."

HOLMES

The rules of war were written. Moriarty did, however, add one interesting footnote upon leaving.

MORIARTY

"If by the winter of the third year you do not see a sign from me then you are free and this pact becomes void. Good day."

WATSON

Then for nigh on twenty years you have lived with this sham?

HOLMES

Yes.

WATSON

And when I wrote of Moriarty's demise it was an untruth?

HOLMES

Yes.

WATSON

What of him now?

HOLMES

[MATTER OF FACTLY] He lives.

WATSON

[AGHAST] No?

END OF ACT ONE

INTERVAL

ACT 2

SCENE: PRIVATE HOSPITAL ROOM

HOLMES

And therein lays my greatest mistake. I was foolish enough to think that Father Time would best him and our pact – ha – our pact would come to nought. He was beyond middle years even then and of weak constitution.

WATSON

I cannot believe what I am hearing?

HOLMES

[EMOTIONALLY] Please Watson, I beg you not to turn against me; not now. You are all I have.

WATSON

But how could you do such a thing? You had no right to keep something of this magnitude from me for so long.

HOLMES

Perhaps I allowed sentiment to cloud my judgement?

WATSON

Who else knows of this?

HOLMES

Just you and I.

WATSON

[RELIEVED] That is something.

HOLMES

I hear vanity in your voice along with relief.

WATSON

[UPSET] How could you say such a thing?

HOLMES

You should think little of the shadow this may cast over your literary self and be alert to the thunder Moriarty can bring upon an unsuspecting world.

WATSON

[AGGRIEVED] Balderdash! I was simply –

HOLMES

[RAISES A HAND FOR SILENCE] Pay little mind to me for I am spent.

WATSON

Do you know his whereabouts?

HOLMES

[SMILING] I knew you would come round!

WATSON

Forgiveness is streets away! His whereabouts?

HOLMES

Until this very day he awaited trial.

WATSON

Trial?

HOLMES

He had taken it upon himself to masquerade under the name of John Robert Bellman –

WATSON

The diamond smuggler?

HOLMES

The very same; a low criminal of little consequence. His time upon this earth was preordained; the odds were stacked against him reaching his three score and ten. No tears will be shed for so despicable a felon.

WATSON

Where did this meeting take place?

HOLMES

Within the confines of Newgate Prison.

WATSON

Where he still resides?

HOLMES

A moot point.

WATSON

[PERTURBED] Very well! You say he masquerades as Bellman? How did you know to find him there?

HOLMES

I happen to know that the real Bellman has been dead for six months. He was despatched by the Brewer gang.

WATSON

The Brewer gang who were thought to be responsible for the theft of the Montclair diamonds?

HOLMES

An unjust supposition; although they are now in receipt of said stones. *[RUNS FINGERS OF RIGHT HAND OVER LEFT WRIST]* One further detail; Bellman was discovered sans hands.

WATSON

Positively ghoulish! I'm guessing that Bellman found rich pickings in Brewer territory, and the gang, by way of retribution, carried out that ghastly deed?

HOLMES

With the added fact that the loss of hands also meant the loss of fingerprints, thus making a positive identification almost impossible. Did I also mention *[DRAWS OPEN HAND OVER HIS FACE]* that his face was splashed with vitriol, further clouding the identification process?

WATSON

It seems that someone went to great pains to make sure that Bellman's identity remained a mystery.

HOLMES

That someone being Moriarty! Bellman's premature demise allowed the professor to step into his shoes. Recall the fact that Moriarty's face is unknown to the authorities and that is why he is able to walk the streets of London with impunity.

WATSON

Then what on earth was he doing in Newgate?

HOLMES

Where better to hide than under the noses of the very people who seek you out? Ingenious.

WATSON

I presume you conversed with him?

HOLMES

[TOUCHES WOUND] Yes.

WATSON

And during that interview you came by that ghastly wound?

HOLMES

[SARCASTICALLY] Your deductive powers show no sign of age.

WATSON

Unfortunately my 'deductive powers' were not sufficient to see through your Reichenbach deception.

HOLMES

My dearest Watson, I do so hope that you will find it in your 'heart' to forgive me?

WATSON

Your tale has flooded my mind with a thousand questions.

HOLMES

You have only to ask to see my hand. I promise I will keep nothing from you.

WATSON
Where am I to begin? *[EXCITEDLY]* I must begin my line of questioning with Moriarty. Why nothing for nigh on twenty years?

HOLMES
My answer at this juncture would be pure supposition at best. Next!

WATSON
Your three year sabbatical! The exploits of which you spoke; were they falsehoods? Did you tell me all?

HOLMES
There was one exception; my near migration to the United States of America.

WATSON
[ASTOUNDED] What?

HOLMES
[LANGUID] A land where true crime is still nourishing and delicious.

WATSON
[DISGUSTED] Really Holmes! In the midst of any criminal act lays a victim, yet you speak as if it were a plate of Dover sole from Simpson's!

HOLMES
[GRIM] I do not create crime! *[QUIETLY]* I am there to sweep up after the fact.

WATSON
I didn't mean to - *[JOVIAL]* So, America?

HOLMES
A golden opportunity. I was within an ace *[INDICATES SIZE*

WITH THUMB AND FOREFINGER] of booking my passage and setting sail. I had received an offer from the Pinkerton agency and their well thumbed missive lay in my waistcoat pocket for nigh on six months prior to the Reichenbach affair.

WATSON

But you decided against it?

HOLMES

With good reason. A familiar face appeared on the horizon – Moran!

WATSON

Colonel Sebastian Moran?

HOLMES

An old adversary, who fortunately is no longer a threat. Through a source close to President Harrison I was presented with valuable data pertaining to Moran's whereabouts. Under the cloak of an alias he had secured a post as security advisor to The White House, no less. Knowing he would spot me in an instant I decided to take to my heels. The rest is known to you.

WATSON

So, Moran was never brought to justice for the murder of Ronald Adair?

HOLMES

Things are never as they appear when Moriarty is allowed to paint a scene in his colours. His forward planning has always been beyond reproach. For your information, Moran did eventually meet with a gruesome end. His just desserts were served to him on a fishing smack sailing from Fleetwood.

WATSON

Good riddance I say!

HOLMES

As we have learned through our many adventures together, things are not always as they seem. *[WORRIEDLY]* I made the mistake of believing that once Moriarty's generals were snuffed out it would put an end to his tricks. *[MAKES GESTURE OF WIPING HANDS CLEAN]* I ignored my instincts! Little did I realise that he had nurtured the ultimate assassin. All of these years and my eyes were closed to the threat!

WATSON

Assassin?

HOLMES

Does the name Schmidt ring any bells with you?

WATSON

I can't say that it does.

HOLMES

Once again I must take you back to events at Reichenbach.

WATSON

Please?

HOLMES

I wish to draw your attention to the messenger. The youth carrying the 'urgent' request that gave issue to your return to our hotel.

WATSON

Yes?

HOLMES

You recall him well?

WATSON

Vaguely. The day was blighted by incident and he seemed to be on the periphery of events. I recall my detailing of him as scant at best.

HOLMES

I would be interested to hear your description of him?

WATSON

Where is all this leading to Holmes?

HOLMES

If you would be so kind?

WATSON

Very well. He was – *[DEEP IN THOUGHT]*

HOLMES

Take your time.

WATSON

No more than fifteen years of age. Fair skinned and dark – no – blonde hair, of average height. I'm afraid that is as much as I can tell you.

HOLMES

Bravo Watson!

WATSON

The passing of time hasn't helped with my recollection.

HOLMES

Perhaps I can help? He was ten years old, of average height for a child of his age and flaxen haired. You may recall he wore short trousers with a distinctive stitching and a scar showed below the hem of the right leg. His name was Dietrich Schmidt.

WATSON

[DIGESTING INFORMATION] Dietrich Schmidt? You are saying that the child we encountered that day twenty years ago was an assassin? *[LAUGHS]* I'm sorry Holmes, but the very thought of a child –

HOLMES

But what of a child guided by malevolence? A child governed by pure hatred?

WATSON

But who would instil such dark feelings in their own flesh
and blood? *[SILENCE THEN REALISATION]* Moriarty!

HOLMES

I told you that he was the master of forward planning did I
not?

WATSON

But this?

HOLMES

The child never stood a chance of respectability with such a
parent.

WATSON

Sickening! I wonder what became of him.

HOLMES

I can tell you exactly what became of him.

WATSON

I am all ears.

HOLMES

Tell me Watson, how old is this chemist?

WATSON

Falkner? Why, I would gauge that he is no more than thirty.
What are you getting at?

HOLMES

And you tell me he is a bright young thing?

WATSON

Yes. Ahead of his field by all accounts.

HOLMES

Like father, like son.

WATSON

You are telling me that Falkner is –

HOLMES

The son of Professor Moriarty!

WATSON

No!

HOLMES

And the ultimate insult; to take the rooms of his father's adversary.

WATSON

But he was a gracious host to you. You arrived in something of an agitated state and he afforded you shelter.

HOLMES

And now you conclude that I am deluded?

WATSON

Not deluded but I think a rest would do you the world of good.

HOLMES

Doctor, I feel your bedside manner requires fine tuning.

WATSON

But your theory re Falkner?

HOLMES

[INSULTED] It is not theory it is fact! You question my analysis? You see a hole?

WATSON

You need to rest my dear Holmes.

HOLMES

[PACES FRANTICALLY ABOUT THE ROOM] This really has been the most savage day. *[COMES TO REST ON THE EDGE OF THE BED]* I would like nothing more than to

smoke an ounce of shag while reading my copy of Mahler's Lieder und Gesange.

WATSON

[JOVIALLY] But couldn't you simply listen to it on a phonograph?

HOLMES

[SNORTS THEN TUTS] Watson!

SFX

DOOR BELL

HOLMES

[WITH A WAVE OF THE HAND] Would you be so kind as to answer the door?

WATSON

But it may be a caller for Falkner?

HOLMES

I will prove the contrary.

WATSON

Very well.

HOLMES

Thank you Watson.

HOLMES BECOMES ANIMATED. MIMES PLAYING THE VIOLIN IN AN ENTHUSIASTIC FASHION. HE SUDDENLY APPEARS LIMP AND RESTS ON THE BED. SEVERAL SECONDS PASS.

WATSON

That's it, you get some rest.

HOLMES

[SITS UP] But first the note.

WATSON

You knew it was a telegram?

HOLMES

It was elementary! *[**HOLMES** HOLDS OUT HIS HAND AND WAITS FOR **WATSON** TO GIVE IT TO HIM]* Now let me see!

WATSON

[SLIGHTLY EMBARRASSED] But –

HOLMES

[IMPATIENTLY] Time is of the essence!

WATSON

It was for me.

*SILENCE THEN **HOLMES** STANDS. HE IS PENSIVE.*

HOLMES

[QUIETLY AND HESITATING] I thought –

WATSON

Yes?

HOLMES

But it was for you.

WATSON

Yes.

HOLMES

Are you needed elsewhere? Please, do not hesitate, not on my account.

WATSON

You know, regardless of how grave the information I have received, I will not leave your side.

HOLMES

[GENUINE EMOTION] Oh Watson, have I really been a hard headed companion all of these years? Tell me true!

WATSON

Not at all - although - you have a propensity to ignore my medical advice.

HOLMES

Ha! And what advice do you wish me to heed?

WATSON

Rest.

HOLMES

[BECOMES ANIMATED] Rest? I cannot rest!

WATSON

I fear for you. You are worn to a shadow.

HOLMES

[ERNEST] How can I bring myself to rest when I carry such weighty news?

WATSON

What news? What is it?

HOLMES

[QUIETLY] War.

WATSON

War?

HOLMES

The unrest between the nations of Europe grows. We have a year at best.

WATSON

A war with whom?

HOLMES

The Rheinlanders.

WATSON

Germans? They are nothing more than sabre rattlers.

HOLMES

They are much, much more. They are a brooding force and since Wilhelm installed Moriarty as his unofficial advisor, I fear for our nation. I really do.

WATSON

The dog!

HOLMES

There is a caper of some magnitude in the offing.

WATSON

Words fail me.

HOLMES

Will you stand beside me in what will surely be our final adventure?

WATSON

How could I possibly refuse such a request from you, my dearest friend? I only hope that these aged bones are up to the task at hand?

HOLMES

Sentiment must be boiled down for I see an evil night ahead of us. If we are fleet of foot then we will have this affair sealed with wax by breakfast. You have your pistol I take it?

WATSON

Yes, I brought it with me.

HOLMES

You sensed an addition to your journals in the making.

WATSON

My instincts are still as keen as ever. What of you Holmes, are you armed?

HOLMES

I have a Derringer concealed about my person. One shot is all

that I will need. I will not rest until I see my nemesis in
lavender.

WATSON

As I have placed myself at your disposal would it be possible
for you to enlighten me as to our destination? Even scant
details would be much appreciated.

HOLMES

Our journey entails a carriage travelling at breakneck speed
from Baker Street to Paddington. From there we board a train
bound for Southampton.

WATSON

Southampton?

HOLMES

Yes! Father and son travel together. We must make haste!

WATSON

If you know of their intentions and their possible hidey hole
then is it not possible to have the local authorities apprehend
them until our arrival?

HOLMES

Southampton is simply their springboard to pastures new.

WATSON

[THOUGHTFULLY] I see?

HOLMES

Falkner is familiar to you so your presence will be invaluable.

WATSON

At the risk of appearing slow witted I presume they are
making good their escape by sea?

HOLMES

Yes. They are passengers on the RMS Titanic.

WATSON

But Holmes –

HOLMES

Come Watson! We have not a moment to lose!

WATSON

I fear our birds have flown.

HOLMES

Flown? *[WITH A BECKONING HAND REQUESTING INFORMATION]* How so?

WATSON

The RMS Titanic from Southampton sailed this afternoon.

*SILENCE THEN **HOLMES** PACES FRANTICALLY. STOPS.*

HOLMES

This afternoon?

WATSON

[APOLOGETICALLY] Yes.

HOLMES

How could this be?

WATSON

Whatever incident occurred before you arrived here at Baker Street has clouded your mind.

HOLMES

[DISTRAUGHT] Sailed.

WATSON

We can only hope that he meets his end in the new world.

***HOLMES** OPENS HIS FINGERS AS IF ALLOWING SAND TO PASS THROUGH THEM. HE SITS ON THE BED.*

HOLMES

Pray that he is sent to Hell before setting foot on American soil. *[**HOLMES** LAYS ON THE BED. APPEARS RELAXED]*

I have always been of a mind that the darkest forces copulated and Moriarty was their issue. What say you Watson? *[AWAITS A REPLY]* Watson? Watson? *[Fraught]* Doctor! Doctor!

JEREMY IS SLEEPING ON THE BED. PROFESSOR DORAN IS SEATED BESIDE HIM, HOLDING A CLIP BOARD.

JEREMY

[A DISTRESSED CALL AS HE AWAKES] Doctor? Doctor? *[JEREMY STIRS]*

DORAN

[SMILING] Good morning.

JEREMY

[SPIES DORAN AND SITS UP ABRUPTLY] Doctor?

DORAN REACHES ACROSS AND REPOSITIONS JEREMY'S PILLOWS.

DORAN

Take your time.

JEREMY

[SCANS ROOM. BEWILDERED] You are?

DORAN

Professor Doran. Remember?

JEREMY

Ah, yes. Dear Professore. *[LOOKS AT WRIST]* Oh dear, I seem to be without my wristwatch. Would you be so kind as to tell me the time – please?

DORAN

[CHECKING WRISTWATCH] 11.30.

JEREMY

[ALARMED] 11.30? I must dress! *[HE LOWERS HIS LEGS OVER THE SIDE OF THE BED. APPEARS WOOZY]*

DORAN

Nice and easy.

JEREMY

I fear I have little choice. 11.30 you say? I feel as though I have slept for much more than two hours?

DORAN

You have. It's 11.30 – Friday!

JEREMY

Good heavens! Then I have been –

DORAN

Sound asleep for two days. Mental exhaustion knows no bounds. Sleep won't do you any harm.

JEREMY

So I have heard. *[LICKS HIS LIPS]* My mouth is dry.

DORAN

I have ordered some coffee and juice for you.

JEREMY

How kind but I think I would prefer tea *[HALF SMILE]* if it is no inconvenience?

DORAN

Not at all. Someone will be along shortly with coffee so I will order it then. Is that ok?

JEREMY

[SMILING] Capital! *[STANDS AND STRETCHES]* You really must forgive me; I had the strangest dream.

DORAN

Is it something that you would care to share with me?

JEREMY

It is of little consequence.

DORAN

[MISPRONUNCIATION] It may help t'tell me about it.

JEREMY

[OVER PRONOUNCED] 'It may help to tell me about it'!
[HEAVY SIGH]

DORAN

Oops! Sorry.

JEREMY

I apologise. It was my fault entirely.

DORAN

Why do you say that?

JEREMY

I'm not really sure. It is as though some unseen force takes
control of my tongue and I find it difficult to stop.

DORAN

I would prefer you to be totally honest.

JEREMY

Then I would like to draw your attention to the beige
overtone in this room. Ghastly!

DORAN

Ha.

JEREMY

Drab, drab, drab!

DORAN

I agree. Not exactly a home away from home.

JEREMY

Precisely. [EYES THE ROOM WITH DISDAIN] I wonder
what I am doing here, in such a place?

DORAN

You are here because you have been unwell.

JEREMY

[PLACES FINGERS TOGETHER AND FORMS A TRIANGLE] And you are of a mind that you can put Humpty back together again?

DORAN

Well, I'm certainly going to try.

JEREMY

[SMILING] Are you up to the task, 'Professor?'

DORAN

I will do my very best with the tools at my disposal.

JEREMY

[SMILING] Oh, well done!

DORAN

First of all you have to come to terms with your problems. Digest as much of the literature as you can and most of all work with me.

JEREMY

[THOUGHTFULLY] Mmm?

DORAN

Please tell me if this is all too much at this time as I realise you have only just opened your eyes.

JEREMY

[RUNS HIS HAND ACROSS HIS FOREHEAD] I will.

DORAN

[ALARMED] Your hand? You've cut your hand!

JEREMY

[LOOKS AT HAND. PUZZLED] You can see it?

DORAN

[TAKES **JEREMY'S** HAND AND EXAMINES IT] Of course!
It looks nasty. Would you like me to get someone to dress it?

JEREMY

Dear me, no. It is but a trifle.

DORAN

Well, if you change your mind?

JEREMY

[SARCASTICALLY] In the absence of my 'tea' perhaps we
should make a start?

DORAN

Wonderful.

JEREMY SITS CROSS LEGGED ON THE BED.

JEREMY

I wonder what you will deduce from this interview.

DORAN

I would prefer to keep it light at this point, more of a chat
than an interview.

JEREMY

[CLAPPING HIS HANDS TOGETHER IN GLEE] A chat?
How cosy!

DORAN

As long as you are up to it?

JEREMY

It would be an injustice to hesitate.

DORAN

Ok, tell me why you are here.

JEREMY

How very direct.

DORAN

If not that, tell me anything you like. *[REFERS TO CLIPBOARD]* All I have here is your recent medical history and a referral from your GP.

JEREMY

And that really will not do! *[FORLORN]* Very well. I feel – *[SILENCE]*

DORAN

Yes?

JEREMY

I feel –

DORAN

Take your time.

JEREMY WALKS TO THE DOOR AND SITS ON THE FLOOR WITH HIS BACK AGAINST IT.

JEREMY

I need a cigarette.

DORAN

Smoking isn't allowed in here.

JEREMY

[EYES CLOSED] Not allowed! *[HEAVY SIGH]*

DORAN

Health risk.

JEREMY

But where better than to risk your health than a hospital?

DORAN

It's still a health risk.

JEREMY

I find this tedious.

DORAN

But I thought you were happy to make a start.

JEREMY

That was before I was informed that there is a smoking ban!

DORAN

What is it in particular that you find tedious?

JEREMY

Having my privacy invaded.

DORAN

But I have to ask questions.

JEREMY

Why?

DORAN

It's my job. I have to get you back on your feet.

JEREMY MAKES SWEEPING BALLETIC GESTURE.

JEREMY

But as you can see dear Professor Doran, I am on my feet!

DORAN

Yes but –

JEREMY

Perhaps the whole thing has been a terrible mistake?

DORAN

Mistake?

JEREMY

[TOUCHES **DORAN'S** SHOULDER] Are you real? You may be an undigested bit of beef, a blot of mustard, a crumb of cheese, a fragment of underdone potato. There's more of grave than of gravy about you, whatever you are.

DORAN

A quote from Dickens isn't going to solve your problems –
and I think it is, 'more of gravy than grave about you.'

JEREMY

[BEAMING SMILE] Well spotted dear heart!

DORAN

I did read a book once upon a time.

JEREMY

Once upon a time? Where all the best tales begin.

DORAN

Where does your tale begin?

JEREMY

My past matters not; it is the here and now that irks me.
[SUSPICIOUSLY] My words are kept safe within the
confines of the doctor-patient relationship are they not?

DORAN

Yes, you are quite safe.

JEREMY DRAWS CLOSER TO DORAN IN A CONSPIRATORIAL MANNER.

JEREMY

There is a figure - a presence – that infiltrates my dreams. I
long for him – for the 'spectre' is most definitely male – I
long for him to step from the shadows and show his face.
This affair has given me many sleepless nights you can be
sure!

DORAN

Who do you think it is?

JEREMY

'He!'

DORAN

Sorry. Who do you think he is?

JEREMY

My dear Doran, do you not see?

DORAN

Tell me.

JEREMY

[WITH VENOM] It is Holmes!

DORAN

[CALMLY] Does he ever speak to you?

JEREMY

[FLICKERING FINGERS] His voice is in the ether, calling to me. You see, he wants to see me fail – and I have.

DORAN

Who has failed? Holmes or Jeremy?

JEREMY

[OPEN ARMS] Ah, there you have it. Would day exist without the advent of night?

DORAN

But you existed before you played the part. How long have you been playing him?

JEREMY

Longer than I care to remember.

DORAN

So, it seems you have identified the shadowy figure in your dreams.

JEREMY

[QUIETLY] Yes.

DORAN

Tell me Jeremy, do you drink?

JEREMY

Not to excess.

DORAN

Is the figure consigned to your dreams?

JEREMY

Alas not. I fear he has picked the lock.

DORAN

Do you have feelings towards the character of Holmes?

JEREMY

Character? Ha! He is much more than words on paper!

DORAN

How do you feel about him?

JEREMY

[COAXING HAND GESTURE] More?

DORAN

Would you defend him?

JEREMY

I have done so on many occasions. I feel this line of
questioning is – oh dear – I feel it is simmering to the boil.

DORAN

I hear that you threw a plate of food at someone for not
sticking rigidly to the words of Conan Doyle. Was that an
example of defending Holmes?

JEREMY

[WICKED SMILE] That was very naughty, I know. The truth
of the tale is that the dish in question was in fact a plate of
Dover sole and the recipient was a mulish script editor. I
apologised profusely; flowers, chocolates, etc, etc.

DORAN

And this was borne out of a disloyalty towards Holmes and his creator.

JEREMY
[WHIMSICALLY] I suppose it was. It didn't help that I was having a beast of a day and – well, you know the rest.

DORAN
How do you feel about that incident now?

JEREMY
I do not make a habit of throwing plates of food.

DORAN
Nonetheless.

JEREMY
I did it for authenticity. For art.

DORAN
Is it not said that authenticity has always been the foe of art?

JEREMY
I am unable to look back over that episode without shuddering. *[HEAVY WHISPER]* There are times when I feel that Holmes plays Jeremy.

DORAN
That's interesting.

JEREMY
And if I falter then both true followers and casual observers alike will crucify me. *[MAKES CRUCIFIXION GESTURE WITH OPEN ARMS]* I have made no secret of the fact that I will never replace Rathbone in the hearts of the public. I have longed to lower my guard but he always looms large. A reminder. A threat.

DORAN
I see?

*DORAN MAKES A NOTE. SHE STOPS AND GLANCES TOWARDS THE
PHOTOGRAPH OF GAYLE HUNNICUT. SMILES. JEREMY IS INTRIGUED.*

JEREMY

Yes?

DORAN

I was looking at your photograph. I – I think I know her.

JEREMY

Then you have no doubt tasted the bitter tang *[GRIMACE]* of
defeat.

DORAN

[REALISING] Oh, I know who she is. She was in an episode
of Fantasy Island. She was very good.

JEREMY

[DISMAYED] There are moments when I despair, I really do.

DORAN

Can't recall her name though.

JEREMY

[HEAVY SIGH] Really? Where is that tea?

DORAN

Can I ask you about being recognised by fans? Does it bother
you? Autographs and the like?

JEREMY

If a body is gracious enough to 'request' my scrawl then I in
turn am gracious enough to comply. However, should just
one more person quote 'that' line from Silver Blaze I swear
on Jupiter's moons that I will bawl! I will!

DORAN

[LAUGHS] I think I know the line you are referring to and I
certainly won't cite it.

JEREMY

[RELIEVED] Thank you. Things may be looking up.

DORAN

How are your moods in general? Up? Down? Tell me.

JEREMY

I am sure, even from this brief consultation that you have already gauged a quotient of my emotions but still you want me to expound.

DORAN

It would help if I heard your analysis.

JEREMY

Where to begin? I can be what is best described as 'the life and soul of the party' and then, if I may borrow from The Crooked Man, 'The smile would often be struck from his mouth as if by some invisible hand.'

DORAN

Are you aware of these events as they occur?

JEREMY

Alas – not.

JEREMY SITS ON THE BED, CROSS LEGGED. APPEARS UNCOMFORTABLE. HE SETTLES INTO A YOGA POSITION.

DORAN

Are you ok?

JEREMY

[WHISPERS] I ache.

DORAN

Ache? Physically?

JEREMY WAVES THE PROBLEM AWAY.

JEREMY

My bones. Sleep, or a lack of it, as I have discovered first hand, can paint the world in strange colours. I am 'certain' it will pass.

DORAN

When not disturbed by dreams do you sleep well?

JEREMY

I am alarmed at 3 a.m.

DORAN

3?

JEREMY

Lines do not learn themselves dear Professor and then there is my make up which is applied with a master's touch. *[TOUCHES FACE GINGERLY]* Not mine! *[FRAMES FACE WITH HANDS]* As you can see, I require more attention than most.

DORAN

I'm sure you don't.

JEREMY

You are too kind. Nocturnal events certainly take a toll on both the mind and body. By lunch I am a spent force.

DORAN

But you continue.

JEREMY

'We' continue!

DORAN

I have been told that you spend an inordinate amount of time on the Baker Street set.

JEREMY

It is my place of work.

DORAN

I have also been informed that you occasionally sleep there.

JEREMY

Your informants must be busy bees. *[COCKNEY ACCENT]*
You've caught me Guv! I'll come quietly.

DORAN

Is it true?

JEREMY

Yes. It has become my safe haven.

DORAN

How do you feel when you have to leave for the weekend?

JEREMY

[WHISPERS] There are times when I scuttle back at night. I am known to the security officers. They turn a 'blind eye.' Am I wrong to do such a thing?

DORAN

Not wrong but I feel it should be addressed.

JEREMY

Why?

DORAN

I understand it is a part of your life, I do realise that, but it is unhealthy to remain at your place of work for 24 hours a day.

JEREMY

Mmm?

DORAN

You have to see it for what it is.

JEREMY

[IRKED] I know exactly what it is! *[DEEP BREATH]*

SILENCE.

DORAN

In order for this to work the first step you take is to accept what you are.

JEREMY

[SARCASTICALLY] And we must abide by the rules and regulations.

DORAN

Once you have done that you will be able to move on.

JEREMY

I find it – *[THOUGHTFUL]* - intriguing, that when I am in my blackest of moods I have blasphemed profusely, no curse left unsaid. Perhaps now my vocabulary, my lexicon, will be bolstered with the term 'manic depressive?'

DORAN

Is that what you feel you are?

JEREMY

If that is what you tell me then I accept it. I will, however, conduct my own rigid examination, but the early signs show a concurrence.

DORAN

And how do you feel?

JEREMY

[EXASPERATED] Oh please! Your bedside manner errs on the side of saccharine. You have dropped a bombshell and –

DORAN

If I can be frank, I don't think it came as a great surprise.

JEREMY

[DEEP THOUGHT] No. You are right. I apologise.

DORAN

Apology accepted but not required. Thank you.

JEREMY

Where next dear heart?

DORAN

Trust. You must trust me. There is no miracle cure but
medication and rest will help.

JEREMY

Medication? Data!

DORAN

I suppose –

JEREMY

[STACCATO] At this juncture I want more than supposition if
I am to place myself in your hands!

DORAN

Ok, I would like to see how you fare with lithium.

JEREMY

[GRIMACES] I have heard dark tales of lithium but please
continue.

DORAN

Before prescribing I would like to draw your attention to its
side effects.

JEREMY

Tell me!

DORAN

Well, dry mouth, overwhelming thirst –

JEREMY

More!

DORAN

- an increase in urination, a loss of appetite; it is also possible
that you may gain weight.

JEREMY

You paint a depressing – *[LAUGHS]* – forgive the pun – but

you paint a depressing picture dear Professor.

DORAN

They are the facts. Ultimately it is all about stabilising your condition.

*JEREMY TAKES **DORAN** BY THE HAND AND PLACES IT ON HIS HEART.*

JEREMY

Is that jubilation or terror?

***DORAN** DRAWS HER HAND AWAY IN AN AWKWARD FASHION.*

DORAN

[AWKWARDLY] So -?

***JEREMY** PLACES HIS HANDS BEHIND HIS HEAD. SEVERAL SECONDS PASS BEFORE HE SPEAKS. HE SITS ON THE FLOOR AND HAS A FAR AWAY LOOK IN HIS EYES.*

JEREMY

I am of a mind to lay Holmes to rest. What say you Professor; is that not a tip top notion? Although, I make no bones of the fact that I find solace when I don *his* uniform. I wish I could turn my back on him but then how would I earn my bread and cheese? Now there's the rub.

DORAN

Maybe a break is called for? A holiday?

JEREMY

[LAUGHS] A holiday? There is no means of escape. He is always there!

***DORAN** CLEARS HER THROAT IN A THEATRICAL MANNER. **JEREMY** FIXES HIS GAZE ON HER.*

DORAN

[UNCOMFORTABLY] Another option is hypnosis.

JEREMY

[QUIETLY] Hypnosis? I see.

DORAN

Although the subject has to be compliant. Have you ever been hypnotised?

JEREMY

No, but I would be a willing 'victim' and I imagine it would be bags of fun. Do your worst dear Professor. I am yours to mould. Ha! Do it!

DORAN

[SURPRISED] Now?

JEREMY

Tut! Where is your spontaneity?

JEREMY CLAPS HIS HANDS TOGETHER AND APPEARS EXCITED. DORAN NERVOUSLY CHECKS WRISTWATCH AND FUMBLES WITH HER CLIPBOARD. JEREMY ROUNDS ON HER AND AWAITS AN ANSWER.

DORAN

Very well.

JEREMY

[LEAPS WITH JOY] Excellent! *[AWAITS INSTRUCTIONS]*

DORAN STANDS. SHE LOOKS ANXIOUS. JEREMY HOVERS ABOUT FUSSILY. THEY GET IN EACH OTHER'S WAY.

JEREMY

Where is the watch?

DORAN

Watch?

JEREMY

Your pocket watch. Your makeshift pendulum that swings to and fro so that it may mesmerise me.

DORAN

[LAUGHING] I may have a chestnut on a piece of string somewhere? Should I look for it?

JEREMY

[SLY SMILE] How droll. Now, where do you want me?

DORAN

Where would you feel most relaxed; bed or chair?

JEREMY'S EYES DART FROM THE BED TO THE CHAIR.

JEREMY

The chair!

DORAN

Very well! Make yourself comfortable.

JEREMY

[SITS] I have a warmth in the pit of my stomach; I call it my Christmas Eve tingle.

DORAN

That's good. Are you comfortable?

JEREMY

Yes. I place myself in your capable hands.

DORAN

First of all I would like you to close your eyes and relax.

HOLMES, EYES CLOSED, ARMS STRETCHED, LOOKS CONTENT.

JEREMY

Very well.

DORAN

I want you to tune into the sound of my voice. It will be the only sound you hear. Relax. Block out any extraneous noise. *[Several seconds pass]* You hear only my voice. Your eyelids are heavy. You feel relaxed. You are as light as air - floating. There is a warm breeze. Do you feel it on your face?

JEREMY

[SLEEPILY] Yes – as light as air.

DORAN

You feel liberated. You are free.

JEREMY

Free.

DORAN

What do you see Jeremy? Tell me what you see.

JEREMY

Leaves – I see autumnal leaves dancing like translucent butterflies. Free of all constraints - uninhibited. I can feel them beneath my feet. It feels good to crush them underfoot. The sound is most pleasing.

DORAN

Are you happy?

JEREMY

Yes.

DORAN

Where are you?

JEREMY

I have entered a kitchen; a farmhouse kitchen.

DORAN

Is there anyone there?

JEREMY

No, it is uninhabited. Wait – I see a cat dozing by the fire. I can smell bread baking. It is the scrummiest aroma. I want to eat it.

DORAN

You can soon. First of all I want you to look around. Tell me what you see.

JEREMY

[PUZZLED] The walls! The kitchen has no walls. It sits in a green field. No windows, no stairs, just a kitchen.

DORAN

Do you feel safe?

JEREMY

Yes.

DORAN

Tell me what else you see.

JEREMY

There is an envelope on the table; a gold envelope. It is addressed to me.

DORAN

Why don't you open it and read it?

JEREMY MIMES OPENING THE LETTER. HE READS IT.

JEREMY

It is blank save for one letter.

DORAN

What is the letter?

JEREMY

W. *[BECOMES HOLMES-LIKE]* The envelope gives nothing away; it is widely available from at least a dozen outlets in the London area. The paper is of a poor quality synonymous with the poorer class of hotel in the Charring Cross district. The ink is of little consequence save to say it can be purchased at the price of one penny a bottle. The signature, ah, the signature was written using a broad nib pen, a Granville. Add to this, it was written by a right handed male attempting to disguise the fact by using his left hand. *[FURROWED BROW. APPEARS PERTURBED]* There is evil afoot here!

DORAN

[CONCERNED] Jeremy, I want you to leave the kitchen. If you exit through the door it will take you to a happy place.

JEREMY

Then I will do so.

DORAN

Take your time; there is no rush.

JEREMY

[EVENTUALLY, A SMILE OF RECOGNITION] Ahhh.

DORAN

Where are you?

JEREMY

I am on Baker Street looking towards my apartments. It is cold here. I feel winter creeping in.

DORAN

Would you like to leave?

JEREMY

I can't. *[TILT OF THE HEAD]* Someone is calling to me.

DORAN

Who is it?

JEREMY

I don't know. There is no light at that end of the street.

DORAN

Why don't you call out?

JEREMY

Hello! Who is it? Show yourself!

DORAN

Do they answer?

JERMEY

No. They are reluctant to show themselves.

DORAN

Then approach them – slowly.

JEREMY

Ah, yes. Now there is the yellowing glow of a gas lamp upon his face.

DORAN

'His' face?

JEREMY

[HORRIFIED] Those eyes, like soot, and the pallor of the skin has all the hallmarks of the grave. I want to stop.

DORAN

[RAPIDLY] Ok Jeremy. I will count backwards from 3 and when I have done so you will awake feeling relaxed. [SLOWLY] 3, 2 –

HOLMES STANDS AND APPEARS ALERT.

HOLMES

Of course, I knew it was you.

MORIARTY

You received my note. It was rather childish.

HOLMES

The letter M – cheap paper – the odour of talcum to mask who knows what – who else?

MORIARTY

This must be the final chapter.

HOLMES

Final chapter? I can only conclude that you have spent a great deal of your time reading penny novels for your vocabulary has become seriously truncated.

MORIARTY

I displease you.

HOLMES

Displease? Tut! Kindly furnish me with an explanation.

MORIARTY

Very well, think of this as your final bow, for in this world of shadows and pain I will afford you no escape. *[LAUGHING]* So you see, Sherlock Holmes, we will forever be entwined – in death!

HOLMES

Amuse me; let me hear how you came to survive the great tragedy of the RMS Titanic.

MORIARTY

Survive? You imply that my status as mortal is still intact.

HOLMES

[SIGH] How tedious. You stand before me, which tells me that you were never on board.

MORIARTY

I hear the cogs clicking into place and the pistons pumping hard in your brain as you teeter on the precipice of reality. Come, Sherlock Holmes; take my hand and join me.

JEREMY APPEARS FROZEN. HE PANICS.

JEREMY

I don't want to go! I want to wake up! *[SHAKING]* Doran, I want to wake up! *[SCREAMS]* Professor!

MORIARTY

Ha, ha, ha, ha, ha, ha, ha!

JEREMY WAKES, ARMS FLAILING, WIDE EYED. HE SITS UPRIGHT WITH A JOLT. HIS EYES ARE FILLED WITH PANIC AND HIS BREATHING HEAVY AND IRREGULAR. DORAN IS SEATED ON THE BED HOLDING HER CLIPBOARD. SHE

*SEEMS IMPERVIOUS TO **JEREMY'S** BEHAVIOUR AS HE CONTINUES HIS CONVERSATION. **JEREMY**, AS IF IN A TRANCE, STARES DIRECTLY AT **DORAN**.*

DORAN

- and yes, that applies to a high volume of patients. I have the exact figures in my office if you would care to see them? So you see, I'm having a darn good go at getting Humpty back onto that wall of his with shell intact.

JEREMY REMAINS MOTIONLESS.

JEREMY

Am I awake?

DORAN

Awake? Yes! We were discussing your progress. It is still early days but we both agreed that the lithium was having a positive effect.

JEREMY

[CONFUSED] But surely - ?

DORAN

Yes?

JEREMY

Pay little mind to my ramblings. *[SUSPICIOUSLY]* So, we were having a tete a tete re lithium?

DORAN

That's right.

JEREMY

Whatever happened to my tea? It wasn't necessary to go all the way to Ceylon for it; I'm sure a cup of canteen premium will do – for now!

DORAN

You want a cup of tea?

JEREMY

My dear Professor, I thought we had already established that fact?

DORAN
I'll get you a cup; I'll see if I can get a biscuit too.

JEREMY
Oh, please! Don't break the bank; not on my behalf.

DORAN
[SMILING] I have a feeling that a few digestives won't bankrupt us.

DORAN MAKES TO LEAVE. JEREMY PLACES A HAND ON HER ARM.

JEREMY
Before you run away please refresh me; you say we were discussing –

DORAN
Lithium.

JEREMY
[AN UNCERTAIN SMILE] Yes, of course. You were no doubt rubbing your hands with glee and celebrating the fact that my health prospers because of its rejuvenative properties.

DORAN
Well, as I said, it's still early days but the signs are –

JEREMY
Favourable?

DORAN
Yes, favourable! *[REMOVES JEREMY'S HAND]* I'll go and see about your tea.

JEREMY APPEARS RIDDLED WITH DOUBT. HIS EYES DART TO THE HIGH BACKED LEATHER CHAIR. HE POINTS AN ACCUSING FINGER IN DORAN'S DIRECTION.

JEREMY

[SOURLY] This really will not do!

DORAN

Pardon?

JEREMY

[OPEN ARMS] This whole charade! It is the purest folly. I fear I am wasting my time and I wish to leave immediately.

DORAN

[TAKEN ABACK] But I feel you are making –

JEREMY

[ABRUPTLY] Good progress? I think not!

DORAN

[SPLUTTERING] If there is something –

JEREMY

[RAISES HIS HAND] If I may beg your indulgence 'Professor' please be kind enough to furnish me with some writing materials; a pen, a sheet of paper and an envelope. I must pen a strongly worded missive to Watson!

DORAN

[SADDENED] Watson?

JEREMY

Yes! I need him at my side! *[LEAPS TO HIS FEET]* The game – is afoot! *[IMPATIENTLY]* Writing materials if you please!

DORAN

Give me a minute; I'll see what I can do.

DORAN WALKS TO THE DOOR AND VIEWS JEREMY THROUGH SADDENED EYES. EXIT DORAN. JEREMY PACES BACK AND FORTH. HE LOOKS ANXIOUS. TAKES THE GAYLE HUNNICUT PHOTO IN HIS HANDS AND LOOKS AT IT. SIGHS. REPLACES THE PHOTO ON THE TABLE FACE DOWN. OPENS THE SUITCASE

*WHICH IS ON THE BED. TAKES OUT A **HOLMES** TYPE DRESSING GOWN AND PUTS IT ON. HE SITS ON THE BED AND TAKES OUT A MAKE UP KIT FROM THE SUITCASE. HE COVERS HIS FACE IN WHITE MAKE UP. HE THEN DRAWS DEEP DARK LINES ONTO HIS NOSE IN ORDER TO ACCENTUATE IT. EVENTUALLY, HIS FACE, NOW A GHOSTLY PALLOR, RESEMBLES HIS INTERPRETATION OF **SHERLOCK HOLMES**. SMILES AND REFLECTS. CHECKS RESULTS IN THE MIRROR, MODIFYING AS HE DOES SO.*

HOLMES

Of course, Doran was known to me and so was unable to win me over.

WATSON

Where is she now?

HOLMES

I have dismissed her on a feeble pretext while we make good our escape.

WATSON

What was it that first alerted you to the deception?

HOLMES

Instinct, my dear fellow, instinct! Theorising is all very well but there are times when one's instincts can not be bettered. *[SMILES]* I feel a short monograph in the making.

WATSON

Can we hurry along Holmes? She may return.

HOLMES

I will be with you presently.

WATSON

I won't rest easy until we are nestled in the comfort of Baker Street.

HOLMES

A truer word never was spoken.

WATSON

Think on, the infernal Lestrade is calling on us at seven.

HOLMES

Lestrade? You must look upon him as light relief in a world of darkness.

WATSON

Yes, but dash it Holmes, your first night at home in weeks; I thought it would be spent by you recounting your solitary adventure.

HOLMES

And a most singular one it is too. If Lestrade promises to remain silent *[PLACES FINGER TO LIPS]* then he is more than welcome to smoke a pipe with us as I recount the tale of the duplicitous Professor Doran.

WATSON

And I am at liberty to take notes?

HOLMES

My dearest Watson; where would I be without my Boswell? I insist that you make copious notes!

WATSON

That's decent of you.

HOLMES

[PATTING POCKETS] Now, where did I put my briar?

WATSON

[EUREKA MOMENT] Got it!

HOLMES

I deduce that it is not my missing pipe that gives you cause to yelp as the celebration would have been much more subdued. Explain – please.

WATSON

There was something buzzing about in my head and I have just remembered what it was.

HOLMES

[SMILING] I would risk a sovereign that there is food in the tale I am about to hear.

WATSON

As a matter of fact –

HOLMES

Yes?

WATSON

- the aroma of steak and kidney was playing about in my nostrils. Mrs. Hudson was preparing it before I left.

HOLMES

When - ?

WATSON

When she had cause to mention that there had been a caller this very afternoon.

HOLMES

And did this caller have a name?

WATSON

He didn't leave his name. Said something about being in town for the day – from Devon or some such place – apparently left his cane behind. Absent minded if you ask me.

HOLMES

Then no doubt this mysterious caller will grace us with his presence – if only to retrieve his belongings.

WATSON

How wonderful it would be if it was the beginning of a new adventure on your first evening at home.

HOLMES

And Devon would be a most attractive proposition at this time of the year. The great Grimpen Mire has always been of interest to me.

WATSON

Grimpen Mire?

HOLMES

A desolate place.

WATSON

Desolate?

HOLMES

Yes, but let us not wallow in melancholia; we must celebrate our reunion forthwith.

WATSON

But I want you to know that regardless of terrain, I would be honoured to stand beside you should the need arise.

HOLMES

Good old Watson; faithful to the last.

WATSON

Well, if there is nothing more I will go and hail a cab.

HOLMES

Just one moment.

WATSON

I'm afraid I must go.

HOLMES

[PITIFULLY] But Watson?

WATSON

[FADING] I am sorry my dear friend but I must leave you now. Farewell.

HOLMES MOVES TO THE HIGH BACKED LEATHER CHAIR. HE RUNS THE TIPS OF HIS FINGERS ACROSS IT LIGHTLY. DUSTS DOWN THE SEAT AS IF FLICKING CRUMBS FROM A TABLE. SITS. HE STRETCHES OUT HIS ARMS IN A RELAXED MANNER AS HIS BODY FILLS THE CONTOURS OF THE CHAIR. A SMILE PLAYS ON

HIS LIPS AND THEN HE IS LOST IN THOUGHT.

HOLMES

Unto this world we come alone *[SADLY]* and here I am. The game is – the game is over. I am but a spent force. My race has been run. *[SIGHS]* Who will shed a tear for Sherlock Holmes? *[CONFUSED]* Who will shed a tear for me? A place amongst the immortals? Or a mere foot soldier? A fancy – consigned to the department of 'do you remember' - ? Did I come to this by happenstance or by spiritual design? I fear I gave too freely, laughed too little, loved too much and died alone. *[RAISED FINGER]* But I will come again – not by resurrection but by way of regeneration. It is folly to dwell on the calibre of creature that will fill my shoes – but come again I will – of that there is no doubt. I will hear the clarion call and I will once again outwit my sternest foe and do all at my disposal to rid this world of evil.

HOLMES *CLOSES HIS EYES AND APPEARS LIMP. MOTIONLESS.*

SFX

BASIL RATHBONE

THE VOICE OF **BASIL RATHBONE** *IS HEARD. THE PHRASE; ELEMENTARY, MY DEAR* **WATSON** *– IS REPEATED OVER AND OVER UNTIL IT OVERLAPS ITSELF AND BECOMES A CACOPHONY.* **JEREMY** *IS KNEELING WITH HIS ARMS OUTSTRETCHED. HE CRIES OUT.*

JEREMY

Let me go *[REPEATS TO A WHISPER THEN CRIES FEEBLY]* please.

END OF ACT 2

CURTAIN DOWN – THE END

The Hound of The Baskervilles

Sherlock Holmes and The Adventure of The Jacobite Rose

www.mxpublishing.com

www.ingramcontent.com/pod-product-compliance
Lightning Source LLC
Chambersburg PA
CBHW081210170626
46811CB00010B/3238